TIL MORNING

A SHORT STORY

B. LOVE

B. LOVE PUBLICATIONS

INTRODUCTION

Hey y'all!

PLEASE READ THIS NOTE!

Latimore and Dana's story was inspired by "If You'll Let Me" but it does not have to be read in order to understand and enjoy "Til Morning."

Til Morning is a SHORT story. It is only 8,000 words. If you are looking for a book that has a beginning, middle, and end this is NOT the book for you. Although Latimore and Dana will have a happy ending, it will NOT be with marriage and babies.

Til Morning is simply my way of showing the layers behind one of the meanest, rudest, and coldest characters I've created in a while. I wanted to show why he was the way he was in "If You'll Let Me" and DASSIT!

Please, please, please, be cautious when starting this story. It will leave you wanting more, but this is most certainly THE END for the Hart brothers :)

Enjoy!
B. Love

Dana finally figured out what it meant to love someone to death. At this very moment, she literally wanted to hunt her husband down and kill him. Dillon wasn't just five hours late for dinner; Dillon was five hours late for their three-year anniversary dinner.

The wine cellar was Dillon's favorite place in their home, so that's where Dana sat for the past five hours waiting for him. In that time, her dinner of steak, fresh green beans, and mashed potatoes had grown cold... its scent turning her stomach out of disgust more than making it rumble in hunger. The tapered candles in the center of the table were halfway burned, covering it with wet wax that had hardened all over again. She had his favorite vinyl record playing at the beginning of the night; now the only sound heard throughout the cellar resembled that of burning logs in a fireplace as the record gently begged her to flip it to the other side.

Her expression had been frozen for so long the tear drops sliding down Dana's face startled her. Lifting trembling fingers to her cheek, Dana brushed the tears away as her mouth fell open. Pressing her lips together tightly, she swallowed hard and stood from her seat. Dana's eyes made a quick sweep of the candlelit table, both plates of food, and the thousand-dollar champagne she'd purchased for their dinner. At the same time, her head lowered and shoulders slumped, and then, the switch happened.

The disappointment she felt with Dillon quickly became anger at herself for thinking tonight would be different. That tonight he'd put her first. That he'd value their vows and marriage above all like he promised he would. Dana let out a tortured chuckle before lowering the top of her body and flipping the table over. Her head flung back... almost in ecstasy... as dishes and champagne flutes broke. As candles dented and food splattered against the floor.

"I only asked for *one* night," Dana seethed just above a whisper, feet feeling weighed down by cement as she trudged over to the wall, "And your ass couldn't even give me that."

Six cherry single rack beds leaned against the wall – holding up hundreds of wine bottles Dillon had collected over the years. Dana's fingers slid down the side of the first rack bed before they wrapped around it completely – pulling it down and shattering the bottles in the process. Her anger gave her a strength she otherwise wouldn't have as Dana took her time pushing the rack beds down one by one. Feeling heavier and lighter after each bed fell. The last one connected with the floor, and Dana returned to the center of the cellar, completely ignoring the multiple brands, flavors and colors of wine that covered her body as a result of the liquid splashing. Inhaling deeply, Dana closed her eyes and allowed the hints of grapes, oak, acid and spice to invade her nostrils. When she'd had enough, her eyes opened, and her fingers slid across the top of Dillon's tasting table.

They'd tasted each other on the table far more than they'd tasted wine. The thought of that had Dana smiling bitterly as she picked up Dillon's most recent possession; a bottle of Domaine de la Romanee-Conti Grand Cru. Dillon ended up paying more for a case of the wine than Dana's parents paid for their home.

He'd kill her if she touched it.

Wasting no time, Dana opened the bottle, took a sip, then poured quite a bit on the ground. Stopping midway, her head tilted as it filled with an even more devious thought. After emptying the rest of the bottle onto Dillon's beige twenty-thousand-dollar rug, Dana grabbed her phone to track his car. Destroying his coveted wine and rug didn't make her feel as good as she thought it would; she wanted to destroy him too. She wanted him to have to look her in her eyes and justify forcing her to spend their anniversary alone.

Dana had the app open and tracking Dillon's location in no time, and as soon as the address popped up what little calmness she had left was gone.

"Again?" she questioned, disgust coating her tongue just as thick as saliva would.

Dillon was a creature of habit. It didn't surprise her that he was at the same hotel as last year. The first time she caught him cheating Dana let it go; this time... she was going to let *him* go.

CHAPTER ONE

D ana

"Fuck this," Dana grumbled, grabbing her ID off the desk and abruptly turning around. "Stupid. Just stupid," she added, turning back to see if the receptionist had returned.

Surprised that she'd made it this far into the bet, Dana tried to find an ounce of pride to cover the shame and disappointment leaving was filling her with. Instead of feeling pride, she felt pain. A lot of pain. Physical pain. With her attention being towards the receptionist's desk, Dana didn't see the tall man walking directly in front of her.

As soon as their bodies collided, Dana fell backwards. Losing her footing, she prepared to fall to the ground beneath her, but the pair of arms that wrapped around her kept that from happening.

Dana's eyes opened, and as soon as they connected with

his, her mouth opened partially in desire. They were a mix of brown and green unlike anything she'd ever seen.

"Leaving so soon?" His face remained expressionless, but there was a hint of a smile in his eyes. Those beautiful eyes.

Clearing her throat, Dana closed her eyes and inhaled a deep breath before opening them and nodding. With a nod, he stood upright, allowing Dana to do the same. As soon as she was planted on her feet firmly, Dana removed herself from his embrace and mumbled a quick thanks before exiting the hotel.

Now she really needed to get out of Decadence.

It wasn't safe here.

Clearly.

Not because she'd almost fallen on her ass, but because it was filled with fine men like brown and green eyes.

With a groan, Dana stomped her foot when she made it outside and saw that her car had been blocked by two others, making her immediate escape impossible. Not wanting to have to search for the owners of the vehicles, Dana walked over to her car, got inside, and prayed they would be coming out to retrieve their bags and park their cars soon.

"This is all your fault," Dana blamed as she dialed her best friend's number. Technically, it was Erica's fault, but Dana was just as much to blame. Had she not spent the past five years obsessively dedicated to every area of her life but her love life, Erica wouldn't have felt the need to do something as foolish as bet Dana that she couldn't go a week without checking in with her job. When Dana lost the bet by calling her office during their vacation, Erica decided to fully enforce her punishment – spending the last few days of their vacation at Decadence, the only twenty-one and up hotel in Memphis, TN.

Erica figured forcing Dana to spend three days in a hotel filled with fine, eligible men looking for no strings attached fun would do her some good, but just the thought of entertaining another man had Dana feeling sick to her stomach before she could even get checked in.

"Don't tell me you changed your mind?" Erica asked.

"Hello to you too, and yes, I have. I don't even know why I agreed to this, Erica, but I'm about to leave now."

Erica sighed heavily into the phone. Her words went in one ear and out of the other as Dana watched brown and green eyes walk out of the hotel. Dana's hand lowered slightly, pulling her hand and phone away from her ear. The sound of Erica's voice pulled Dana out of her trance as she called her name.

"Yea?" Dana answered, watching brown and green eyes walk to the car that was in front of hers.

"Are you even listening to me?"

"Yea," Dana lied, watching him open the door of his backseat. He grabbed his bag, but when he noticed her sitting in her car he tossed the bag back onto the seat and closed the door. "I'll call you right back."

Dana disconnected the call and opened her door, irritation rising by the second. Brown and green eyes leaned against his car. He crossed his arms over his chest and his left ankle over his right ankle. This time when he smiled, it was a small smirk that lifted both corners of his mouth. The smile that was in his eyes earlier had vanished as he looked her body over slowly and carefully.

"Is this your car?" Dana asked, placing her right hand on the hood of her car.

"Yea."

"Can you please move it so I can leave?" Dana looked back at the car that was parked behind her before saying, "You two have me blocked in."

Latimore shook his head as he pulled the cigar that was tucked behind his ear out. He waited until he'd pulled the lighter from his pocket and lit the cigar to say, "No, I can't."

Dana's chuckle was more out of anger than amusement as she asked, "Why not?"

"Because if I move, you'll leave. I don't want you to go."

He talked in a blunt style that grated on her nerves, but his voice... his voice... those eyes...

"Why not?"

"I won't know that until I talk to you."

Dana smiled, hating herself for loving his desire for her. Still, it wasn't enough to make her stay. It was actually more motivation to leave. She'd done without a man or sex for five years. No man would come into her heart, life, or pussy and fuck up the peace singleness and celibacy had given her. Especially one as fine as brown and green eyes. One whose smile was so confident she was sure he was the kind of man who was used to always getting what he wanted.

Except now.

He wouldn't be getting her.

Dana's smile fell as her nostrils flared. She tried to remain in control of the moment and her emotions by controlling her breathing. After pulling in two deep breaths, Dana softened her voice as she asked, "Will you please move?"

Brown and green eyes shook his head, as if she was inconveniencing him, and slowly made his way over to her. But he didn't look at her. He didn't bless her with those beautiful eyes. Not until he stood directly in front of her. Their eyes locked for seconds that Dana admittedly didn't want to end. She broke his gaze, only to take in the rest of his features.

His dirty brown and black dread locs were arm pit length. Dana could see a few tattoos peeking up out of the top of his shirt, and his left arm was almost covered with them. He had pink medium sized lips that took Dana's mind to a place it should not have been going to with a complete stranger. And he had a stubble covered strong, square jaw that accentuated his perfectly chiseled high cheek bones.

Yea, he was definitely the kind of man that was used to getting what he wanted.

"No," he spoke finally, and Dana had gotten so caught up in taking him in that she'd completely forgotten what they were talking about.

"What?"

"I said no. I'm not going to move."

"Then I'll call for security and they will make you move."

He chuckled, and there was something about the sound and sight of it combined with him stepping even closer and licking his lips that made Dana's heart throb. Pulse race.

"I'm Latimore Hart, baby. There is no man on this earth that can move me."

Her nerves choked her. Muffled her. There was something dangerously attractive to her about a confident man, and the longer Latimore towered over her, unfazed by her threat, the more she felt the tension melting between them. The more she felt herself softening towards him. Dana reminded herself that she needed to keep it together, because moments earlier just the mere thought of letting loose was enough to shatter her.

There was no way she could handle a weekend of sex with a stranger.

No matter how satisfying that sex could be.

A shudder shot through her body at the thoughts of connecting it with his.

With Latimore.

Latimore Hart.

Coming to her senses, Dana lowered her head and took a step back and away from him.

"I'm not surprised that you're attracted to me, but I'm not your type." Dana looked towards the hotel entrance. "I'm not this type. I don't do casual sex and one night stands..."

"Then why are you here?"

Her eyes returned to his, and the disappointment in them couldn't be ignored.

"I don't know."

Latimore nodded and took a step back.

"Fine. Leave."

There was something about Latimore telling her to leave that made Dana want to do the opposite. She watched as he walked to his car, fighting the urge to tell him to wait. How dare he give her what she wanted and somehow make her feel bad about wanting it at the same time?

"You don't tell me to leave. I'll leave when I'm good and ready. I don't need your permission, Latimore."

His walking stopped at the sound of her saying his name, but he continued to his car and opened the door.

"Whatever, sweetheart. I'm about to move so you can leave."

Was this a joke?

Some kind of reverse psychology?

"Maybe I don't want to leave. Maybe I'm staying."

Latimore turned in her direction, looking just as confused as she felt.

"Do what you want. I don't care anymore. There are far too many women here for me to be wasting my time with you."

Dana couldn't keep the grunt that escape in before she yelled, "Well fuck you!" and kicked her tire. The sound of Latimore laughing before he slammed his door only irritated her more, causing Dana to snatch her purse out of her car to finish checking in.

No one told Dana Green what to do – not even if it was what she wanted to do.

CHAPTER TWO

L atimore

Even with her throwing herself at Latimore he wasn't interested. She'd literally given him her room card wrapped with her panties and his shaft was still soft. It wasn't like Latimore wasn't attracted to Trina. Or was it Tracy? He couldn't remember. She just... didn't have anything on the woman he'd met hours earlier.

This wasn't Latimore's first trip to Decadence, but it was the first time any woman had ever thrown him off his game. He visited the hotel so much he had enough points to rack up fifteen free nights at the hotel. In Latimore's mind, Decadence was like heaven on earth. Not only was he able to come in and have as much sex as he wanted without having to worry about pregnancy, diseases, or calling the morning after... but he also didn't have to work too hard to secure his women during his stay.

If anyone was at Decadence, there was a silent expectation already set in place – all guests were there for sex.

But that wasn't the case with the clumsy woman from earlier.

She wasn't as easy of a mark as Latimore expected.

That was cool, or at least Latimore thought it would be. He was sure he could replace her. Easily. But four hours and ten other women later, Latimore wasn't sure if that would be possible. The clumsy woman had piqued his interest in a way that no other woman ever had.

"Latimore?" Latimore looked at Tamara. Or was it Trina? No. Tracy. "When can I expect you to come?"

Latimore scratched the side of his nose as his phone vibrated in his pocket. He pulled it out, then excused himself from the table in the bar as he answered Logan's call. His brother's newfound love and marriage was also a reason this visit to Decadence wasn't going as well as he expected it to. Logan had never agreed with Latimore's way of living or how he treated women.

Latimore hadn't really ever cared about his brother's opinion of his lifestyle or anything else for that matter, but the happiness and peace that Logan was filled with on a daily basis because of his relationship with Nola had Latimore wondering if the way he lived was worth it. If single-ness was worth it. If having a different woman in his bed once a month was worth it.

"What's up?" Latimore answered, hoping Tracy or whatever her name was would get tired of waiting for him and leave, but he knew that more than likely wouldn't happen. He had a reputation at Decadence, one that led every woman who heard of him to believe he'd leave her well satisfied.

"It's official. Heard the heartbeat today. Nola's pregnant. My baby is about to have my baby."

Latimore's heart dropped and his knees buckled. He may not have had a desire to settle down and have kids of his own, but the thought of becoming an uncle brought tears to his eyes.

"For real? Congratulations, bro. We have to celebrate next weekend."

"Yea, I'm going to need you to have a kid that my son can grow up with." Logan paused, letting his request settle in. "Like we did."

Latimore's hurt, though years old and deeply buried, had become a wound that only love could heal. Sadly, he had absolutely no desire to try to love again.

"You know how I feel about that, Logan."

Latimore looked towards the table in the back of the bar and Trina waved at him with a smile.

"And I thought seeing me with Nola was changing your mind?"

Scratching his scalp, Latimore made his way back over to the table. This wasn't the time or the place to have this conversation, so he figured it was best to end it.

"I'll hit you up when I get home Sunday. We'll link up."

Instead of waiting for Logan to agree, Latimore disconnected the call as he slid back into his seat.

"I thought you were about to leave?" Latimore checked, trying to mask his irritation.

There was no way in hell he could have sex with her or anyone else tonight. Not with his brother's love, happiness, and growing family on his mind. Sex wouldn't give him a release. It would only confuse him more. Have him thinking it wasn't enough. It would have to be enough. There was no room in his heart for love.

Not anymore.

"I was hoping you would come with me." Her hand went to his thigh and she squeezed. "Right now."

The door of the bar opened and closed, and Latimore didn't even have to look up to see who it was. He could feel her. Feel the hairs on the back of his neck rising up. Feel his heart race and his dick harden. Latimore looked to the left, fighting back a smile at the sight of the clumsy woman.

Latimore couldn't stop looking at her beautiful face. Her curvaceous body. She was blessed with the type of beauty that was intoxicating – a salve seeping through to his scarred soul. There was a danger that stemmed from the way she was built, one that had Latimore battling his attraction.

Her sleek, jet black bob was freshly laid, and it matched the black dress and lipstick she wore. Those heavily slanted brownish black eyes that Latimore swore penetrated his soul looked him up and down as her bow shaped lips opened slightly. She had the most perfectly sculpted high cheek bones he'd ever seen in his life. And if her smooth walnut colored skin tasted as good as it looked Latimore definitely wouldn't have minded settling down for her.

Settling down? He'd just met the girl. Well, he hadn't really even met her yet. She'd bumped into him once, and was now engaged in a heavy gazing contest with him. Neither of them was in a rush to look in each other's eyes. They were both too busy taking in every other part of the other.

Now she was taking the time to get reacquainted with

his features. Like those dirty brown black dreads. That sandy brown skin. Those artistic tattoos. That strong jaw line and scruffy beard. Those pink lips. Those brown and green eyes. Damn him and those eyes. She seemed to be fine until she looked into his eyes.

The clumsy woman lowered her head and walked over to the bar. She sat down, pushing a few strands of hair behind her left ear. Latimore watched as her leg began to shake. It was clear that she was on edge about something, and as much as Latimore didn't want to care... he did.

Latimore slid Tracy's panties and room card back to her across the table.

"What's your name, sweetheart?"

"Terica."

With a nod, Latimore stood.

"You enjoy your night, Terica."

"What is that... are you... seriously, Latimore?"

Ignoring Terica, Latimore walked over to the bar and sat next to the clumsy woman. Close enough to feel the heat of her body transfer to his. Close enough to have his nose pleasantly assaulted by her scent. Latimore called for the bartender and ordered himself another shot of whiskey.

"Can I get you something?"

The clumsy woman looked over at him, eyes tight in irritation. She disliked him already. Latimore didn't blame her. He'd practically dismissed her earlier. That hadn't been his plan. As soon as her body connected with his, Latimore wanted to claim her.

Even if it was just for the weekend.

But as soon as she ruined his fantasy, Latimore did what he did best – became an asshole to give her a reason to not like him and push him away. That was a lot easier than handling a woman's rejection because he simply wasn't her type or good enough.

He'd had enough of that with Gina.

The longer Latimore stared at her the softer her eyes became, but she didn't answer until she looked away.

"Tequila."

CHAPTER THREE

D ana

"How long are you staying?"

Dana accepted her drink before answering Latimore. Truth of the matter was, she needed time to accept the fact that she was still at Decadence. That she was sitting next to Latimore. That she hadn't been able to get him out of her thoughts since he freed her car and gave her the room necessary to leave. It didn't matter how much Dana tried to convince herself that she was staying so she wouldn't have to hear Erica's mouth and not because she was too damn stubborn to leave simply because Latimore told her to... there was a second truth that tormented her.

There was something about Latimore that intrigued her, and she was dying to figure out what it was.

"Til morning." Dana downed her shot before looking

Latimore over. "I was supposed to stay until Sunday, but I don't think it will take me that long to figure it out."

Latimore let a few seconds pass before asking, "Figure what out?"

Dana couldn't afford to be distracted by love and the allure of a happily ever after for a life that had been everything but a fairytale, but for one night... one night... Dana had finally made up in her mind to surrender to her heart and her body. To prove to herself that Dillon wasn't the only man who could take or break both. If she gave access to herself to another man, it would have to be on her terms. What better time and place than Decadence and Latimore Hart? A place known for its one night stands and a man who Dana was sure had more than his fair share of one night lovers.

Dana let out a quiet chuckle as her head shook softly.

"Why my heart fell for you the second you kept my body from hitting the ground." Latimore's head shook adamantly, but before he could speak Dana turned in her seat and added, "I'm not saying I love you or no shit like that. I don't even know you." She chuckled again and looked around the bar, unable to ignore the woman that was staring daggers at them. "I barely even like you." Dana sighed and ran her fingers through her hair, messing up the middle part she'd spent two minutes perfecting. "All I know is when I looked into your eyes..." She turned back in her seat and looked straight ahead. "I can't explain it. There's nothing I can compare it to."

Dana expected that to run Latimore away, so she was surprised when he said, "Why don't we go to the back of the bar and grab a table?"

As if he expected her to agree, Latimore stood and extended his hand for her to take. Dana did, cursing herself silently as her nipples hardened from the contact. They went to the back of the bar, and Latimore allowed Dana to get comfortable in the booth before he sat next to her. Close. Leaving no space between them.

Every fiber of her being warned her. Whispered that she ignore the ache in her heart that grew for him. It was when he rested his arm atop the table and looked deeply into her eyes that Dana knew exactly what it was that drew her to him. It was pain. The same pain Dillon had given her. The type of pain that couldn't be hidden or ignored.

Latimore licked his lips as he pushed her hair out of her face, causing her to smile when he admitted he wanted nothing in the way of his view of her beauty. His desire was blatant. By no means was Dana blind to his attraction. She just... wished like hell she would have been able to ignore her own.

"I cannot offer you my heart or that I will value yours," Latimore made clear with the same sincerity the average man would use to confess his love for a woman. "That's not why I'm here. I'm only good for sex. It will be best for you if you stay away."

"You made me move over here to tell me that?" Latimore's head shook but he remained silent. "Then what do you really want to say to me?"

"It's not what I want to say to you that matters. More so what I want to do."

Her body betrayed her as it began to want him before he even made his proposal.

"And what exactly do you want to do to me, Latimore?"

Latimore's hand went to her cheek. He caressed it with his thumb before using it to pull her closer to him. With his eyes, he asked for permission. When Dana closed her eyes and nodded, Latimore covered her lips with his. The kiss started out soft, then hard, then soft again. His mouth possessed hers, demanding that she give him just as much as he gave her in return.

And she did.

She did.

Their tongues wrapped around each other, and Dana hated to admit it, but she enjoyed the taste of him.

A lot.

So much so that she whimpered and bit down on her bottom lip to keep herself from protesting when he pulled away.

"I want to fuck you," Latimore confessed. "Slowly at first." His stare lowered down her body slowly. Pausing at what she figured were his favorite parts of her. "Then hard enough to make you beg me for mercy."

Every ounce of her loneliness, desire, fear, and excitement melted together, creating a surge of overwhelming need for him.

This was what she needed. No, this was what she wanted. And for once, Dana wanted to go after all that she wanted. No fear of hurt or scars from wounds left in Dillon's wake would keep her from enjoying everything Latimore had to give. But there was one stipulation.

"I can only agree if I don't feel like we're total strangers. I have to know you mentally and emotionally before I can know you physically."

Latimore's head began to shake as he put some space between them.

"That defeats the whole purpose of coming here. If I wanted to get to know a woman..."

"You don't even know my name!"

"Then what is it?"

Dana's eyes rolled as she smiled and shook her head. She paused before whispering, "Dana. Dana Green."

Latimore nodded and sat back in his seat.

"I don't usually compromise, Dana. It's either my way or no way at all." He scratched his chin as he looked her over intently. "But for some reason, I don't too much care about maintaining my rules with you." Breaking their eye contact, Latimore looked around the bar for a waitress. He used two fingers to tell her to come to him, and when she nodded in acknowledgement Latimore returned his attention to Dana. "I'll give you access to me on one condition; you must promise me that when you leave tomorrow morning you'll be okay with never seeing me again."

Dana waited until the waitress came and took Latimore's order, an entire bottle of whiskey and tequila, before she agreed.

They started with the basics about each other. Family backgrounds. College and career facts. Latimore was serving as COO of his family business, Hart Express Soul Food. He was also opening a chain of barbershops and beauty shops for his cousins to run in Memphis, Atlanta, Chicago and Denver. Dana wasn't surprised of his desire to open a few clubs and strip clubs, but he planned on waiting until he had the rest of his businesses established before taking that leap.

Dana confessed that she wasn't the entrepreneurial type. She didn't mind working for someone else. In fact, she enjoyed the fact that she didn't have the pressure of running a business and being the boss of others. Dana was perfectly content with her position as Advertising Executive and planned on keeping it within the same company until she retired.

Their conversation remained light for a while as they

covered their favorites, fears, dreams, and goals, but things took a turn when marriage and kids were brought up. They both were thirty and neither had children. It was easy for Dana to admit that she wanted some but Latimore had a harder time letting that truth out.

"Never really said that out loud," he confessed, taking another swig of his whiskey straight out of the bottle.

"Why not?" Latimore remained silent for so long Dana added, "I told you about my failed and hurtful marriage. You can't tell me why it's so hard for you to talk about your desire for children?" His head shook. "Does it have anything to do with why you come here?" He nodded. "Did a woman... did she hurt you?"

Latimore tried to lift the whiskey to his lips again, but Dana wrapped her hand around his wrist as best as she could and kept his hand on the table.

"You can trust me, Latimore. I won't judge you, and I won't tell anyone your business."

Dana listened intently as Latimore told her about the last time he ever tried to have a serious relationship with a woman. Gina. He met her in college, where love and settling down were the last things on his mind. In love's usual fashion, it didn't care whether Latimore wanted to experience it or not. Love bombarded its way into Latimore's heart and life as soon as he met Gina.

Problem was, Gina had more willpower than Latimore. Sure, she liked him, but she loved his money more. She loved his status and family reputation more. Instead of seeing him for who he truly was, Gina focused solely on what he had to offer.

Six months into their dating, Latimore was head over heels in love and Gina was pregnant.

Problem was, Latimore didn't know that Gina's baby wasn't his.

It didn't matter how much his parents warned him to be careful or how much Gina's baby looked like the man she swore was her best friend. Latimore refused to deny his son or even take a DNA test. For six months, he grew attached to Latimore Junior. He even went as far as to propose to Gina to give his son the same loving environment with both parents that he was blessed to grow up in.

Gina's best friend, Brandon, returned from Iraq and shattered Latimore's entire world. He found it strange that Gina wanted to randomly elope a week before, but he figured she was finally seeing what she had in him – a loyal, loving, honest, romantic, faithful provider and protector that was willing to give his life for her and their child. But, the truth was, Gina was using marriage to keep Latimore after the truth came out.

When Brandon returned, he asked to see his child and went as far as to threaten Gina with an attempt to receive full custody of Latimore Junior if she didn't come clean.

She did.

A DNA test was done.

And the family that Latimore was so proud to have was immediately ripped from his hands.

Ever since, Latimore made it his mission to never give a woman access to his heart or his seeds again.

And he'd been doing a pretty good job. Until he met Dana. She had a way of forcing him to search his own heart while she snuck her way inside. Logan's newfound love, marriage, and happiness didn't make it better either. Or his request for his brother to finally settle down and start a family of his own.

"I want no parts of a woman's heart," Latimore ended,

tightening his grip around the whiskey. "Can't even protect my own. I refuse to be responsible for yours."

Dana watched as Latimore lifted the liquor to his lips. A part of her wanted to tell Latimore that she was willing to risk her heart if love was a possible reward, but those words wouldn't come out. Maybe it was her recollection of her own tattered heart and the damage done to it by love, but Dana couldn't pull herself to try and convince Latimore that love was worth the risk. Just when she'd made up within her mind to let thoughts of them go, her heart spoke to her on its behalf, and she smiled when she realized...

"You're not a bad guy, Latimore." She took his hand into hers and placed it in her lap as his glossy eyes found hers. "You don't come here because you're heartless. You come here because it's the only way you've learned to use your heart less." Latimore tried to pull his hand out of hers, but he stopped when she tightened her grip. "But... I think... my heart is safest with you, because you wouldn't put it or me through the pain you went through." Dana loosened her hold on his hand, giving him the chance to pull away, but he didn't.

"If pain is the common thread we share, maybe it will be what keeps us from ever hurting each other. And maybe it won't. Maybe we'll be too paranoid to see where this can go. I don't know. All I know is..." Dana inhaled deeply as her eyes watered. She looked away, unable to believe the words that were about to fall from her mouth. "All I know is... if you want it... my heart and my body are yours. But, but only til morning."

Latimore stood. He extended his hand for hers as he mumbled, "Then you have mine."

CHAPTER FOUR

L atimore

This was dangerous, but Latimore didn't care. Nothing would stop him from getting his fill of Dana Green. Especially now that he'd shown her the inside of his heart – a place no woman had seen in close to nine years. The truth left him raw. And drained. But he would make sure he used all the energy he had left to make this a night Dana would never forget.

His goal was to make her cum as much as he could before she had to go, and Latimore kept reminding himself of that as he watched her undress. Piece by piece, her clothing fell until she stood completely naked before him. Earlier when they kissed, Dana opened her mouth to him easily, and he prayed her bottom set of lips would be just as inviting.

"Your body is so beautiful I have to take the time to honor it," Latimore acknowledged, leaning against the dresser. "Are you comfortable with stimulating me visually before things get physical?"

Dana's head lowered briefly as she smiled. When it lifted, she nodded.

"Yes. What do you want me to do?"

Her submission and desire to please him turned him on more.

"Get in bed." She did. "Spread your legs." She did. "Beautiful." Dana's hands covered her face, causing Latimore to smile. "You changing your mind?"

Dana inhaled deeply. He'd learned that she tried her hardest to tame her tongue. Careful of how quickly she spoke. Dana lowered her hands and shook her head.

"No."

"Spread those lips. You're already so wet for me." Latimore's fingers ached to touch her, mouth to taste her, dick to fill her, body to cover her. "Touch yourself."

She did, and he grew so hard it hurt. Her opening spilled a wet welcome as he watched her. Lust and need for her filled every part of him, so much so that he couldn't think of anything else that he'd ever wanted more. Latimore sheathed himself and walked over to the bed. Yes, they'd talked about her being on birth control, and being free of STD's and HIV was a requirement before they could even check into the hotel, but there was no doubt in Latimore's mind that Dana had the type of pussy to drive a man crazy, and going inside of her raw would only draw him deeper under her spell. He crawled towards her, taking in her rapid breathing and trembling body.

"Are you sure about this, Dana?"

"Yes," she whispered, pulling her arms up and grabbing the pillow.

Latimore made his way between her legs. The stubble of his beard tickled her thigh and she closed both, causing Latimore to use his hands to spread them wide. He could smell her arousal, and it was almost enough to have him leaking and shuddering before he even entered her. His thumbs parted her wet folds, making room for his tongue to tantalize and tease her, but he didn't do so just yet.

Dana's eyes fluttered shut as she bit down on her lip. Her eyebrows wrinkled in frustration. In need. Latimore smiled when she entangled her fingers with his dreads and coaxed him to finally taste her. He found her slippery clit and worked it until her legs wrapped around his neck. The gasp that fell from her lips as her pleasure built motivated him to lick, suck, bite and kiss her more.

She arched into him as he ate her, feeding her goodness to him even more. It wasn't long before Dana surrendered to the sensation that filled her body and came.

Latimore lifted himself and covered her body with his. Skin to skin, chest to chest, Latimore paused at her opening, giving her one last chance to change her mind. Her hand went to his neck and she nodded again, giving him all the confirmation he needed. Slowly, Latimore entered her. Her moan, half pleasure and half pain, fueled and egged him on. It reminded him that he was the first man she'd given herself to in five years, and that reminded him of his goal – to make her cum. But something snapped inside of him as soon as she began to suck him in. Something that made him want to feel the pleasure of that first stroke inside of her again. Over. And over. And over. Again.

Pushing those thoughts far back into his mind, Latimore pressed into her harder. Deeper. Filling her to the hilt. Her walls closed around his entire length, keeping him secure and snug in a warm, euphoric embrace. Dana arched her hips and matched each of his thrusts. Her moans became just as loud and steady as the sound of the headboard rattling and their bodies connecting. Latimore covered her mouth with his to taste, savor, and swallow every whimper... every gasp... every moan of his name and her pleasure that fell from her lips.

She was so eager to respond to his touch. Her wetness spilled freely as she heated and tightened against him. Dana's nails slid down his chest as her lips began to tremble. No longer was she able to fuck him back. She became paralyzed by the pleasure of having him inside of her. Her hands went to his stomach, and she tried to use them to push him out of her as her climax began to rise.

"Take all of me," Latimore moaned, hardening and speeding up his pace. "Every fucking stroke."

Latimore lifted her hands above her head and put his mouth to her ear. For once, he wanted to let a woman know that she felt just as good to him as he felt to her. His breath was hot and hard against her ear before he panted her name. It was as if pleasing him pleased her, because the more he moaned the wetter she became.

Not wanting this to be over soon, Latimore raised himself from her chest. He was about to change positions, but Dana wrapped her legs around his waist, pinning him inside. Latimore tried not to focus on how good she felt, but everything about her and their moment consumed him. From the way she felt to the way her and her body sounded. The way she looked. How her breasts bounced and swayed like two watches, placing him in a trance that would soon leave him hypnotized.

He squeezed and caressed them, gently at first, then with a bit more force.

She liked force.

Her walls began to close against him, and that was all it took to send Latimore over the edge. They came simultaneously, each seemingly fueled by each other's pleasure. Latimore removed himself from her and fell back onto the bed. His heart rate and breathing were both high as his eyes closed in relaxation and relief. Latimore's body went into immediate recovery mode, but he would soon be ready for part two and hoped Dana would be ready. She made it clear that she would be when she cleaned his softened shaft with her tongue.

CHAPTER FIVE

D ana

It was crazy. She'd known him for twenty-four hours and was having the hardest time saying goodbye. Spending the night with Latimore was more than Dana could have ever hoped for. The sex was amazing, but what she enjoyed most was what happened in between their sessions. After every time Latimore entered her, a piece of the wall that he was using to guard his heart was stripped away.

He talked more.

Shut down less.

He smiled.

And cracked jokes.

Confessed fully to his desire for love, marriage, and children, but was just as honest about his fear of being hurt again. And when their bodies finally forced them to shut down, Latimore held her as they both drifted off to sleep.

He woke her up with the best lazy sideways sex she'd ever had, then they went and had breakfast together. Now they both were standing next to her car avoiding each other's eyes.

"Well... thank you," Dana muttered, releasing a loaded sigh that had Latimore stepping towards her.

"For what exactly?"

Latimore's voice was low as he used the tip of his finger to lift her head by her chin.

"Showing me that my heart still works."

With a small smile, Dana filled the space between them and placed a gentle kiss to his cheek. She let her lips linger there for a few seconds in stillness before walking behind him to her car door. Latimore opened it but stepped in front of her so she couldn't get in. Dana's smile widened as she asked, "We're back to this again? You're not going to let me go?"

Latimore's head shook as he cupped her cheek and used it to pull her into his chest. When he first kissed her, her smile remained on her face, but the second she felt the tenderness of his lips her smile fell. The finality of their time together set in, and Dana was no longer in the mood to joke.

"You did the same for me." His voice was just above a whisper, and the thick passion that it was filled with caused Dana's newly working heart to ache. "And I will forever be grateful to you for that, Dana."

"I know a way you can repay me."

Latimore's head tilted. He took one step away from her just to take two steps towards her.

"How is that?" His arms wrapped around her, nestling her comfortably in his chest. "How can I repay you?"

She wanted to tell him by letting her love him and be loved by him, but she couldn't find the courage to say that. Instead, she said, "By... using your heart. And not letting fear keep you from loving and being loved."

Latimore remained silent, waiting for her to say more. When she didn't, he nodded and released her.

"I can do that," Latimore agreed, stepping to the right and letting Dana get inside of her car. With one hand holding the door, Latimore rested the other on top of her car. "Did you mean what you said at the bar? About trusting me with your heart because I'd never force you to feel the pain I've sustained?"

Dana nodded. She chewed on her lip as she looked away, giving her eyes time to dry.

"Yes."

"You uh..." Latimore tapped the top of the car as he thought over his words. Dana returned her eyes to his. "You... you sure you want to take that chance with me?"

Her cheeks raised as she smiled. Dana's head lowered as she chuckled quietly.

"You said til morning..."

"I didn't say which morning. You sure you want to take that chance with me or not?"

Dana got out of her car and made her way into his arms.

"Absolutely," she whispered into his chest, losing herself in the sound of his heart beating.

Dana had no idea how love would make its way through two shattered hearts, but she was looking forward to every morning she'd get to spend trying to figure it out with Latimore at her side.

THE END